Praise for
Letters to My Lover
From Behind Asylum Walls

Written from an asylum, these epistles provide something more "delicate and wrathful" than the expectation that our interned speaker has a tenuous grip on reality. Instead, we witness moments of wisdom and lucidity made possible because the strength of Sweet Jane's love for Eleanor is greater than the weight of her trauma. These poems guide us through the questions we must ask about how memory and isolation work after a severe tragedy, in order to determine which truths we are most invested in preserving, perhaps more than which are worth discovering.

–KRISTI CARTER, AUTHOR OF *COSMOVORE* AND *DAUGHTER SHAMAN SINGS BLOOD ANTHEM*

Robin Sinclair's poetry reveals, in careful construction, the movement in grief. This is Robin's homage to the human body. They are ruminant, reflective, hauntingly tender when they speak, "I wonder what all of this will look like when completely healed." Here is gentle longing, they shape it as both touch and desire. I believe Robin when they write, "There are bones in dirt they're sure of if they just knew where to dig." The body is alive, "viciously creating a future." Here, we lean in to listen to the music of all that we don't remember happening. The music is as real as it is indelible, and it speaks to you, "There's so much hunger here, my love. They feed us well, but not what we need, and if I don't get out soon I fear I may starve." And if this isn't the truth, I don't know what is.

–TANYA SINGH, AUTHOR OF *HEAVEN IS ONLY A PART OF OUR BODY WHERE ALL THE SICKNESS RESIDES*

Read the cycle of poems here in Robin Sinclair's *Letters to My Lover From Behind Asylum Walls* and be immersed in its passages of rawness, brutality, wry humor and truths and you will find it as foreboding, palpable, and as freeing as when you first read *The Bell Jar*. Unlike *The Bell Jar*, Sinclair's collection is wholly of our times, scraping as it does beneath the messy surface, seeing life as it is when the carapace of wellness and serotonin blankets is ripped away and we see the damage done. Read this book because it is so vital to exorcising many ghosts—yours, mine and ours, past and present!

–G.E. SCHWARTZ, AUTHOR OF *ONLY OTHERS ARE: POEMS, WORLD, THINKING IN TONGUES* AND THE FORTHCOMING *MURMURATIONS*

LETTERS

TO MY

LOVER

FROM **BEHIND**

ASYLUM

WALLS

LETTERS

TO MY

LOVER

FROM **BEHIND**

ASYLUM

WALLS

ROBIN SINCLAIR

ROCHESTER, NY

Book and cover design by Nina Alvarez

For permission to reprint portions of this
book, or to order a review copy, contact:
editor@cosmographiabooks.com

For more information, visit
CosmographiaBooks.com

ISBN-13: 978-1-7322690-3-3

Letters

The Script.	March 14, 2003
The Bridge.	March 21, 2003
The Funny Thing About Laughter.	March 28, 2003
Waiting.	April 5, 2003
The Chariot.	April 12, 2003
He Is Real.	April 19, 2003
Chocolate Covered Cherries.	April 19, 2003
The Nurse With The Hole In Her Hand.	May 28, 2003
The Shotgun Story.	June 4, 2003
The Land of the Wayward Specters.	June 11, 2003
The Girl With The Clipboard.	June 18, 2003
The Way The Martyrs Die.	June 25, 2003
They Sewed Me Together Like a Doll.	July 4, 2003
A Picture of Your Mother.	July 14, 2003
A Letter From The Gray Dawn.	July 24, 2003
Whispers At A Wake.	August 1, 2003
The Need.	August 12, 2003
The Nightmare.	August 22, 2003
I'm Sorry.	August 29, 2003
I, The Moon.	September 5, 2003
Barcode Girl is Dead.	September 12, 2003
The Secret.	September 19, 2003
The Turn of the Chamber.	October 1, 2003
I Remember.	October 9, 2003
The Spade in the Hill of Dust.	October 20, 2003
The Crows.	October 30, 2003
The Last Morning.	November 5, 2003
The Last Night.	November 5, 2003

Content warning:

Mental illness, self-harm, rape, and suicide.

Copies of Patient Correspondence.

The Script.

Eleanor,

It's been a month, and
I've earned a pen, paper, and
what they call *privacy*.
A doctor whose name I can't seem to etch permanently
believes writing letters to you may help.
Perhaps he's reading.

I don't remember it happening.

I remember biting just outside the arch of your foot
before dropping my head,
I remember your taste and how
we laughed until we cried because
you pulled me into you so hard that you
broke my nose.

I remember being at a restaurant with my aunt —
she'd eaten more than half of what was on her plate,
then
sent the food back because it tasted funny,
I recall her refusing to pay and someone mentioning
this not being
the first time she'd done this.

I remember how easy parallel parking was on my
driver's test
and thinking to myself about how every 80s sitcom
made it
out to be the Curse of Davy Jones, toppling
desperate youths overboard to plummet toward the
bottom of the sea
over and again.

I remember watching Alfred Hitchcock late at night,
a black and white television with a
hand-knob for channels.
I remember my birthday and my mother's old car.
I remember everything about you.
I just don't remember it happening.

They say they're here to heal me, to treat me.
There's a cure for what I'm feeling right now,
it's called *specifics*.
Funny how no one seems able to fill the script.

Yours Truly,
Sweet Jane.

The Bridge.

Dear Eleanor,

If it were any other,
I would fear your heart would break.
But it is you. Mine and
theistic and knowing.
They were focused on you again today,
trying to make you my bridge to them.
The arrogance.

If you were a bridge, you'd start on the shores
of Cap-d'Ail, arch into the skies and end abrupt
in the haze of heaven and storm-cloud,
half-built and stony like a crumbled aqueduct.

I told them that you love me, and that I love you,
but that it was knowledge and not emotion.
It was belief in the ocean by someone who's never
seen it,
except that I've felt you before, but feel little
now.
It's a man who is blinded by a flash of lightning
and eventually forgets his wife's face,
not because of indifference,
but because he's simply forgotten what it means to
see.

I know you will understand.
You're out there, somewhere.
Waiting for a flutter of color in your chest
and in mine.

Wait for me.

xoxo
Sweet Jane

The Funny Thing
About Laughter.

Hi Eleanor,

Dr. Osinope is a thick Greek man
with thick Greek breath.
He sits awkwardly close for a man
whose purpose is to study my mind,
which can be examined from a foot away
or across the room or even on the telephone
while I sit with you in a hotel in Portland.

I accidentally spit on him today.
He was murmuring about memory and
I was lost in the blackness of the forest
on his forearm,
some dainty Disney character stumbling over roots
and vines of dark and wiry hair.
I imagined them getting into my mouth somehow,
and I started to scowl and spit.

Some landed on Dr. Osinope.

When I'd realized what had happened, I
began these bellowing belly laughs,
laughs I haven't laughed in what feels like forever,
like the broken nose laugh or the time

letters to my lover from behind asylum walls

we dressed up like scarecrows on Halloween
and waited on the porch like props for
trick-or-treaters,
staying so still even when we had to pee,
coming to life when they rang the bell.
Just for the laugh.

For a moment, I felt better,
but Dr. Osinope couldn't understand
what I found funny.
He left me sitting at a table,

scolded with silence. They punish with mystery.

I'll write again soon.

Yours Truly,
Sweet Jane

April 5, 2003

Waiting.

My Eleanor,

He was in the halls again last night.
I know it was him.
Like a mother hearing her daughter's cries in a
sea of a thousand voices,
I know his footsteps as if my own,
He stopped outside my door but didn't enter.
He just waited.
Breathed.
Stared at the wall as if he could see me through it.
Never blinking. Never moving. Never speaking.
Waiting.

I could see him through the veil as clearly as he
could see me.

Call someone, Eleanor.
Get me out of here.

Sweet Jane

The Chariot.

Eleanor,

It's a dreadful chore, really,
staying alive.
For whatever reason, some people who don't care
about living tend to continue to do so.

Like me.

Some days, I don't actively want to die,
I'm simply apathetic to the thought of life
and all its seemingly absent "wonder" and
"splendor."
The longer I'm here, the more absent they feel.

Other days...those are obvious.

Reason to live, they repeat like a pop song,
The bones of a beloved emperor, and I, the
motionless chariot
trying to drag them home with forced hope.

It's tedious,
eating, washing, speaking, waking, walking.
Dull tasks performed by dullards themselves,

keeping meat clean just-because.
And here I am, given makeup like a milk-bone,
plastic spoon under hawk's eye,
my head patted by people paid to care about my
pulse.

When I force my thoughts not to wander to past sex,
old movies, or how books should have ended,
and I listen to the droning on of strangers,
desperate to fill a shallow pool
that seems to always be draining through a thin
crack at the bottom,
I do it out of trust.
When I spit vague blue bubbles of toothpaste,
make lists of blessings,
say *how that makes me feel*, or swallow mashed
potatoes, I do it because
I trust you, who isn't here,
to know my future's worth
better than I do.

Yours Truly,
Sweet Jane

January 15, 2003

Patient: ███████████████
Date of Birth: ███████████
Schizoaffective Disorder, 29

Comorbidity of Major Depress
Personality Disorder 301.83

Possible Comorbidity of Disa

History and Exclusions.

Short-term delirium has bee
of symptoms. Patient Histor
disorders left untreated. F
Standard serology workup ex
physiological cause of symp
triggers.

tient suffers long-term M
a, visual hallucination
with verbigeration, suicida

Also conducted Woodcock-Joh
shows normal sensory and mo
psychotic state.

tient previously treated
derline Personality Dis
er 1999 – August 200
treatment. Prev

He is Real.

My Sweet Eleanor,

I saw him again,
in flashes still, as if
he only exists between blinks when my eyes flutter.
I was almost able to forget.

He looked dirty, cold, angry.
It's only for a moment, but a moment is long enough.
Doctor Dickless spent an hour patronizing me,
telling me he's not real.
It's funny how when you ask someone to define real,
they look at you like you're insane.
But I am insane. That's why I'm here,
or at least that's what they let me believe
since no one wants to tell me anything.

I know he isn't there to be touched,
reasoned with, or shown how to love and to forgive.
If he were, I would wash him,
hold him while he cries about his dead wife,
or about being dead and his wife being alive.
We could heal each other within these cold,
real walls and leave together as friends.

But he isn't.

He's there in fragments of light,
hiding behind those floating dots in my eyes that
whisk themselves away on the Fourth Horse
when I try to catch them.
He can never hear me, though I hear him
moving in the halls.
I can never touch him, though I fear his
thumbs pressed against my throat in the night.
That's why he's real, Eleanor.

We are trapped here, together.
Both alone.
And he is real.

Yours Truly,
Sweet Jane

PS: Open my next letter in the morning time.

Chocolate
Covered Cherries.

Good morning, Eleanor.

It's been so long since I've
been able to say that to you,
always waking an hour later than the world I know,
always innocent like white sun on the Black Sea.
I envy your welcome to the world,
never angry, or begrudging, or fearfully clinging
to a secret dream you'd never want us to know.
Your eyes simply...
open.

I had a dream of my own,
of chocolate covered cherries,
Have you eaten any lately?
Every day for a week all I've been thinking of
is that taste,
smooth and tart and sweet.
I wake up shy from thoughts of silken syrup,
sticky lips and hot tongue trying to make the
sensation linger.
When I get out, I'm going to eat nothing but candy
every day for a month -
they don't serve it here.

They serve those powdered potatoes
and canned green beans.
The potatoes frighten me because they
aren't real food,
and when they chide me for it like a child,
I blame the meat.
I tell them I'll never get my pudding
if I don't eat my meat,
but they never get the joke.

There's so much hunger here, my love.
They feed us well,
but not what we need,
and if I don't get out soon
I fear I may starve.

Dream of Me.
Sweet Jane

The Nurse With the Hole in Her Hand.

They watch me, Eleanor.

They watch me eat,
leering at my nibbles and counting the times
my tongue
gnaps mashed potato
from the roof of my mouth.

They watch me shower,
my dirt and sweat is judged before
it spins away,
And I am protective of my dirt.

They watch me piss,
and I wonder what they watch for.
Dribble or direction of wipe, or does the dainty
nurse huff the smell of me
when I'm not looking. I wonder why she snickers.

They watch me sleep.
And while I sleep, they record my breath.

They put me in Quiet Room for two days and
took away my pen and paper for a month,
restricted to my room except for meals and mockery.

letters to my lover from behind asylum walls

I didn't realize why until they showed me.
They tape me, Eleanor.

I was stuttering and rambling hard against a wall,
some part of a word I couldn't get past,
over and again.

Someone touched me and I stabbed her with a pen.
Went straight through that webby part between
her thumb and pointer finger.
It became an affair.

So they punished me.
They tape me, and they watch me,
and they fuck me with their tiny plastic cups
and their tongues and their eyes and
pens of their own,
and they punished me for being sick
with an illness they won't say aloud.
They said it was for my own protection,
but I don't remember stabbing myself and
didn't remember stabbing *her* until they showed me.
I didn't mean it.

I cannot heal without you.
It is all I feel and know for sure.
And they punished me by taking you from me.
I hope the next time I have one of my spells,
I aim for someone's eye.

Just kidding.

xoxo
Sweet Jane.

The Shotgun Story.

Dearest Eleanor,

I wanted to talk about other things,
but they wouldn't let me.
They just kept coming back to the shotgun story.

What I said. How I felt. Who I blame.
What I see when I remember.

I see the brown faux-wood door to the bathroom,
and I see the light peeking out from under it.
I always hated how yellow
the world was in your bathroom
and how it only got uglier when it bounced off of
the pink tiles and dusty white caulk.

I was disconnected from you, which frightened me.
I felt the thin thread between us as you lost
control,
like trying to breathe back in my own mist in the
winter.

I blame myself for
not knowing your heart well enough.
I blame your mother. I blame chance.

letters to my lover from behind asylum walls

I said that we could fix anything as long as we were
together,
and then I watched across the silence for you to
turn back and wave,
coming home and growing nearer or
setting course toward some unknown blackness.

They seem fascinated with the silence when
I tell them.

Then I see the brassy knob jiggle and I can still
hear
the lock turn before the door opens.
You fade in like a ghost, apprehensive about the
world beyond the bathroom,
and hand me the gun.

Sweet Jane

The Land of the
Wayward Specters.

Dear Eleanor,

The halls we walk,
the rooms we eat in,
we're in a place between today and tomorrow,
some hotel floor closed down for superstition,
our eyes made of cobwebs and dust.
The walls teeter over us, the moment where the moon
comes out
but the sun is still shining,
and the sky is confused as to who to believe.
I forget everyone's names,
but names are a useless passion. We're
angry ghosts, silent and white linen draped on
bones.
If you went to the muddy shore
where life on this world began,
and built a city of stone,
towers spiraling into ashy red skies,
you'd find me there, in
the land of the wayward specters,
haunting, hungry, weeping, dying,
but never fully dead.

Sweet Jane

The Girl With
the Clipbord.

My Eleanor, I pity them.

Line drawn in
sand of flesh brings something,
anything
coiling toward the front of her throat
 and backs of her eyes.
 She is free here
 – Alone, but free.
The girl with stripes laughs like a normal girl
should.

Leather strapped wrists,
tube-tongued pulchritude
her Castle Cséjthe raped by hunger.
They wheeled her here to ask her why
but find her over the oval again.
The girl with the sunken eyes misses human touch
like all of us do.

Ballpoint hate scratches
into spreadsheets
at night she hears our voices
sees our soiled flesh
our blood on her latex glove

our stories on the stage of her eyelids
played by a cast of her own.
She may join us one day in the sunroom.
The girl with the clipboard is the saddest girl we
know.

The girl without reason,
Sweet Jane

The Way the Martyrs Die.

My Eleanor,

I hated being alone,
but I may hate social sessions more.
Prolonged group therapy with the inane and
intolerable.
They want me to make friends, but
I can't think of anyone I want to know
that isn't you.

I watch them as they pander to one another,
hateful or lusting or desperate.

Have people always been this way,
so concerned with how others perceive them
that they make their projections their realities?

I can't imagine a martyr on a cross
or perhaps beginning to burn,
being surprised at the end of their story,
their last thoughts being the greater good as
their flesh begins to bubble like some primordial
muck.

No, they're imagining the thoughts of others,

the memory of their sacrifice living on through
story and song for generations,
names etched in stone walls that line the roads of
time.
They are grinning as they scream,
pretenders still pretending, like we all do,
trying not to show the gurgle of sickness from our
shame.

Martyrs die with ambition,
fulfilled and jubilant as they
cry in agony, slinking with a smile from
one life into the next.

I'm longing for someone real.

Yours Truly,
Sweet Jane

They Sewed Me Together
Like a Doll.

Dear Eleanor,

They asked me again,
What do you remember?
I told them that I don't remember anything
because that's exactly what they'll tell me -
nothing.

That's not how memory works.

They showed me a tape of my third week here.
I was naked, my arms bandaged.
It was supposed to awaken and connect,
but all I could wonder was why was I bandaged,
and why hadn't I shaved in so long.
My only epiphany that I hadn't noticed my arms all
this time,
not until I saw the tape.

They say I couldn't be sedated because of the blood
loss,
but they couldn't restrain me because of the wounds.
*My mind didn't understand that my body was
too weak to move.*
He snickered when he said that, Dr. Osinope.

I don't get what's funny, which I suppose is fair.

They sedated me,
risked killing me to get rid of me.
They sewed me together like a doll.

The scars are thick now,
jagged and cruel in form and
I wonder what all of this will look like
when completely healed.

xoxo
Sweet Jane

July 14, 2003

A Picture of
Your Mother.

My Lovely Eleanor,

I'd mentioned in a recent Group
that you always carried an old photo of your mother.
It never occurred to me to wonder why.
I noticed the weathered edges so many times,
but never asked for the story of the photograph.
The story of your mother, though, is one I know.
You struggled your entire life to forgive, my love,
so brave in the face of your own pain,
valiant and steady, looking anger in the eye,
Perhaps I was just so accustomed to not asking about
her.

Osinope told me to speculate,
and I imagined it as a part of some spell of
protection.
I saw you sitting at your alter after midnight,
colored candles lit and acacia leaves in your palm.
I was just left with more questions.
Protection for you?
Protection for her?
And where did you learn all of this?

Maybe it was your way of making peace after all,

and I'd never bothered to learn the tale of
the most significant act of love in your life.

Do you remember when I'd finally asked you why
you call me Sweet Jane,
and you told me about a night we were
sitting in your car,
smoking cloves and kissing hard
while Cowboy Junkies were playing on the radio?
I couldn't remember the evening, but you
never let it make you insecure. You know me.
You know I adore every moment I get to
live within your life,

and that I simply don't remember based on merit.

Whatever the reason for the photograph,
I should have asked,
and I'll ask to know every piece of you
when we are finally together again.

Love,
Sweet Jane

July 24, 2003

A Letter From
the Gray Dawn.

Good morning, Eleanor.

It is a gray dawn, with hot anvil eyes, and
if I dig myself into you hard enough
you will be here

half real like an echo in an empty hall,
like fragments of memory that peek into the now -
quick flashes that I know didn't happen,
but aren't any less real,
and if I could hold them here, outside of my mind
for just a moment more,
the world would see them, too.

I fixate, viciously creating a future,
and yes, the doctors may be sinners in the hands
of an angry God.

It is a night,
behind a tiny home
somewhere without locks or fluorescent light -
we sit in plastic chairs near a fire pit,
the yard glowing warm like the yellow sun of
childhood Spring

It is a Someday,
when we're gray and
lined like handwritten scripture –

we sit content to lose our memories
and minds

together, glowing brightly, in and out of time.

See you in the future,
Sweet Jane

Whispers at a Wake.

My Eleanor,

I overhear them speaking,
like whispers at a wake
hoping the others won't hear your voice
not sounding sorrowful

...The medication is working...
...Still not the progress I'd hoped for...

Today I'll be a victim and
tomorrow, a liar.
I wander through empty ritual,
open to their promises.

I've been moved to Social Rooming.
They want us to catch butterflies together in a
prison
and less privacy is somehow a gift.
A girl with a barcode tattooed on the back of her
neck
introduced herself as a recovering murderer.
She hears voices, but isn't allowed to tell me what
they say.
Something about her brings out the Holden Caulfield

in me.

Osinope asked me today if I was sure he was real.
For the very first time, I felt he'd been listening,
and for the very first time, I was more sure than
not.
He shouldn't whisper.

xoxo
Sweet Jane

The Need.

My Eleanor,

That Barcode Girl wept today in Group, forced
to tell a story that made her feel alone.
She refused, said she knew what it would do to her,
said she knew the memories in the air would
break her,

but they raped her.
They didn't pin her down, a forearm across her chin,
pushing harder as she quietly cried;
they simply shaped her thoughts with words until she
laid on her back
and found herself somewhere else.
When it was over, she lost her breath,
started drifting,
wobbly-drunk from failed escape and
the wave of an almost forgotten feeling.
They carried her away,
sobbing as she screamed, "I need her."

A girl named Kim once whispered to me through a
telephone
that she needed me.
It turned my chest to tar,

like that feeling you get walking into a courtroom
or climbing the stairs to your apartment, knowing
there will be an eviction notice on your door.
I didn't need Kim. I didn't need anyone —
I had always felt complete on my own until I met
you.

I don't remember what my response to Kim was,
but it was more than likely a lie.
Someone who is whole never needs to be untruthful.

Today I woke up feeling what I've known I feel,
but haven't felt in some time.
I was terrified. I missed you.
I was hopeful,
and fought to hang onto the edge of a dream, but
could only recall an empty country road
I did not recognize. Dusty dirt met the pavement
just below the guardrail.
Beyond that, I've lost the image.

I hope to see you soon.

Sweet Jane

August 22, 2003

The Nightmare.

Eleanor,

Last night I dreamt of cornstalks
and a man who isn't real.

He stepped into the first row
and the soil turned to ash.

As he thrust into the crops
A fire followed close behind

He was searching without eyes
stalking, hunting for his prey

You hid me from the monster
told me that you'd have his head

I promised you my silence
as I watched you clench your fists

He had cut the field in half
with a growling wall of flame

When I peeked from tender shadows
You were on the other side

He turned his head and saw me
hollow holes as black as coal

Then he smiled and moved toward you
You were fearless, you were God.

I couldn't see it happen
He had vanished with the fire

The stranger took you with him
and the world was slightly wrong.

The cornstalks - melted plastic
simulacra in their place

I woke up, cold, regretting
Learning how to feel again.

Yours,
Sweet Jane

I'm Sorry.

My Sweet, Forgiving Eleanor

I'm sorry.
Please forgive me.
I was weak to the warmth of her words
and the loneliness within these walls.

I didn't ask her to,
she just started touching me,
kissing me.
But I didn't tell her not to.
I never told her to stop,
and I should have.

I don't love her,
I don't feel anything that is particular to her.
I just felt desperate.
Desperate for a real voice saying real words
that I wished were yours,
whispered or moaned in a motel bed
near a small beach town with a boardwalk.

It did feel good,
I won't lie,
but it also felt like that thick tar on my heart,

knotting my gut even as I came.
But I did. And it was the first time I've been held
in so long
and the first time I was touched by someone else,
touched without cynicism or violence.

Please forgive me.

Still yours, truly and completely.
Sweet Jane.

I, the Moon.

My Delicate and Wrathful Eleanor,

I lay splayed across a sun turned into itself –
        the brightness in the universe
upside-down and burning my nakedness.

Bring to me your wickedness –
        bring to me forgiveness,
I ask you to become judgment
for the sake of the future.

You alone will define me –
        perhaps only by this sin,
but my face is the same that kissed yours

crying, as we burned your starry queen –
        your six cups always empty,
your *auto-da-fe* for another's trespasses.

Absolve me here –
        as done before,
two fools' bodies dipped in perfumed water,

oil of chrism sealing our sins into one another –
        and through the tower's yellowed windows of
trust,
I will look in upon a loop of life and
forever repent.

We both teeter on the edge of the sword –
        you, my priestess,
and I, the moon.

Forgive me, Eleanor –
        and return to me,
your open heart,

Sweet Jane.

Barcode Girl is Dead.

I can only imagine your agony – envisioning
the filth of another in and on my flesh.
I can feel through the sky
and walls and into my breast
how your pain turned to rage.

But did it turn to revenge?

Barcode Girl stood up at breakfast – without a word
and started to run.
She ran through the large glass doors that remain
unlocked
for those of us in Group, and ran down the hall.

I followed her through the door – I watched her
until she turned the corner toward the stairwell.
She lowered her head and
dove from the top step with purpose and

On the landing of the staircase that separates us
from the world – her skull
hit with the sound of a stack of books
in an empty library.
She crumpled in on herself.

I could see in my mind – the faded green lines and
numbers under her hair, wrinkling like a soiled bed
sheet tossed away.
She fractured her own skull and broke her neck, and
the intern that rolled her onto her back apparently
made matters worse.

She died 17 minutes later – surrounded by
people who didn't know her favorite song
or if she liked to dance when she was alone
or if she believed in god.

I would never assume you'd be so wicked –
truthfully, perhaps presumptuously,
I assume that you've already forgiven me,
because that's the nature of your love, our love,

but I couldn't feel better unless I told you –
an image
of you, furiously sobbing
and reciting incantations,
had crossed my mind.

But I know you, my love – I know you
better than that, and now,
more than ever, I know
that I must find the answers.

Yours,
Sweet Jane.

September 19, 2003

The Secret.

Oh Eleanor,

I am burnt pages begging for return to my author
desperate for a quill pressed into my flesh
a hundred thousand lines
      the lore of me
      scrolled across my back
until I'm whole again.
Wilted, I know nothing of hiding.

And they are the ones with the secret,
A secret I've discovered.
An Emperor without wisdom
They do not tell me
because they do not know.
They await,
they are waiting for me.

Soon, dearest.
Sweet Jane

The Turn of the Chamber.

I'm sorry it's been so long, Eleanor.
Something is happening to me – something
I'm confronted with in everyone around me – the

one who insists on a boy's name,
I can't recall which,
hides hurt behind hardened skin
hides the memory of a tender touch
surrender and betrayal,
They ignore His words and try to treat Her.
We hide our sympathy.

The one who poisoned herself
blew out a vein, desperate for calm,
hides the scar, hides the nub of her ring finger.
They saved her arm and her life and
she carries a towel, pretending
to be washing dishes or her face.
We hide that we know, that we've seen it.

Carol is dying and hides porno in her mattress,
extra desserts in the bathroom.
We hide them until we can give them to her.
I hide a book that I stole from Osinope's office
in a vent at my bedside.

It explains that my mind has hidden me,
has a word for when I allow myself to be found,
doesn't tell me the cause.
They hide their fear of what it might be.

Perhaps it was the guilt,
Perhaps it was the sound of the skull and the floor,
Perhaps it was the medication,
Perhaps it was you that somehow pulled the trigger.

Click,
Sweet Jane

I Remember.

My Eleanor,

I remember.
I remember being truly alone.
The barrel, the brick, and the brine,
saltwater in the corners of my mouth
breaking my concentration with the taste.

Every breath was desperation on the pages
I've torn from my spine.

I remember.
I remember the sound of nothing.
The mirror, the meaninglessness of me,
what it felt like to have all of my memories,
some visions overpowering others, unmaking my mind.

Unwoven by a single use of power or lust.

I remember.
I remember it becoming clear.
The lockbox, lacuna, and laugh,
epiphany of refusing to be rewritten
and having the means to be erased.

I would not be alone, slipping in and out of the sea
they sail upon.

I remember.
I remember your voice.
The whisper, the wonder, the wilt,
how you picked off dead petals and
spoke of the future as if you'd already seen it.

Cool water and hot tears, you were reconciliation,
as if you'd been there all along.

Eleanor - I
I might enjoy getting
what I deserve.

Yours Truly,
Sweet Jane

The Spade in the
Hill of Dust.

My Eleanor,

Somewhere,
down below the spade in the hill of dust,
beyond the chemicals that create momentary abandon
past the places with air remorse could breathe
just under the tips of the roots, dug deep into time
beneath the bones of all regret
there is choice.

Without a flicker of dogma or excuse –
all knowing, all seeing,
pure and apathetic.
They offer me salvation,
chalky and bitter on my tongue,
or a musty exhumation
threatens that I'll come undone.

Delicate hand on an ageless casket,
I have made my choices.
I have made my choice.

Yours. Truly.
Sweet Jane.

October 30, 2003

The Crows.

Dearest, Loving Eleanor,

Do you recall our first night in the field,
stumbling over roots
and each other
the cloak of familiarity yet to be?

It's Autumn and I can think of nothing else,

the season exhaling through branches,
making leaves quiver and chatter like old friends.

the sound of subtle escape
easing from your throat like old jazz.
That same voice I hear confessing,

a curve grazed with teeth and tongue,
a smile running its length,

The lost island behind your ear
where secrets would land in years to come and

the devil's den between chin and breast.

Keep our soil under your nails and

listen for the crows.
They're watching.
They're coming.

Sweet Jane

The Last Morning.

Sweet Eleanor – it is happening.

Coward hints at opprobrium
like you built our home in Nod
"I understand," I said.

My whispers to mastema,
the morning the books dropped
"I can't seem to recall," I said.

There are bones in dirt they're sure of
if they just knew where to dig,
"I'm sorry," I said.

Subtle voices, flashing fragments,
all the hauntings in my house
"There's nothing more," I said.

It was a strange transition,
from where I was to who I am
"It's thanks to you," I said.

They smiled, shuffled papers,
printed copies and signed names.

"Let's go downstairs," he said.

There are other inked names needed
and a name of whom to call
"I'm alone," I said.

Not alone, darling.
Sweet Jane.

PS: I hope my next letter is the last. If it is,
open it right away.

The Last Night.

My Love, My Lover, My Eleanor.

As I write my final letter to you,
I realize that I have nothing but faith
that the others have ever arrived.

Pills within pillow,
now hidden in an envelope.

I ignored the nurse's feigned farewells,
did not say goodbye to the girl with sunken eyes
as she coughed into the water

Stared at the stairwell,
scrubbed of blood and bone.

I thanked the cook, thanked the orderly,
thanked the television set and the free books,
thanked the heavy fan that drowned out the
witching hour cries.

Forgotten secret cigarette,
slipped behind my ear and under my hair,
save it for the interstate.

Meet me Saturday at dawn,
at the tree beyond the crops.
I have to hear the leaves
scratch against one another,

to see for myself that the stalks are real
and the crows remain.

There are bones in dirt they're sure of
if they just knew where to dig,
"I'm sorry," I said, and meant it,

though they did not
know how.

Subtle voices, flashing fragments,
all the hauntings in my house
"There's nothing more," I said, and I meant it,

though they did not
know how.

This is the ending I've chosen,
with you,
with who I truly am.

Yours, truly.
Sweet Jane

5.70

sion 296.3, Borderline

associative Disorder 300.15

n excluded as possible cause
y reveals possible long-term
amily history unknown.
cluded authoritative
toms and substance related

.

ajor epression with bouts of
s an aracusia, loss of focus
l thoughts.

nson and Brown ADD. Patient
tor function when not in

for Major Depression 296.2 and
rder 301.83 by Dr. Monroe,
. Patient voluntarily
ously prescribed Gabapentin

Discharge Notes.

The author wishes to thank G, EB, DG, LMH, & the Ghost.

Special thanks to *Pidgeonholes*, who first published "Barcode Girl Is Dead" in their tenth volume, "Verda," May 2017.

Unyielding gratitude to *Yes Poetry*, who published "The Shotgun Story" in their October 2018 issue.

If you've enjoyed my work, the most precious sign of support you can give is to share my work with others. Send them a book or a link to a poem. Let them borrow yours and read it for free. I don't care. Just share art. If you steal a bunch of my stuff, maybe buy me a drink one day. -R.

Links:
www.sardaa.org
www.suicidepreventionlifeline.org
www.CosmographiaBooks.com
www.pidgeonholes.com
www.RobinSinclairBooks.com

About the Author

Robin Sinclair is a queer, genderqueer writer of mixed heritage and mixed emotions, currently living in New York City. Robin's work has been published in various magazines and journals, including *Gatewood Journal*, *Shot Glass Journal*, *Black Heart Magazine*, *Red Bird Chapbooks*, and *Yes Poetry*.

Subscribe to Robin's mailing list:
RobinSinclairBooks.com

Robinsinclairbooks.com/dirt